For Alice, Archie and my husband James – the inspiration for 'Daddy'.
S H

For Tilly with love x.
N E

EGMONT
We bring stories to life

First published in Great Britain 2016
by Egmont UK Limited,
The Yellow Building, Nicholas Road, London W11 4AN
www.egmont.co.uk

Text copyright © Sam Hay 2016
Illustrations copyright © Nick East 2016

Sam Hay and Nick East have asserted their moral rights.

ISBN 978 1 4052 7715 0

A CIP catalogue record for this title is available from
the British Library

DO NOT WASH THIS BEAR

by **Sam Hay**

Illustrated by **Nick East**

EGMONT

My Daddy is not very good at doing the washing.

He makes my T-shirts titchy.

He turns my vests pink.

And he **disappears** my socks.

So when he wanted to wash Bear, I cried:

"No!"

But Daddy didn't listen.

"Bear smells," he said. "Bear is muddy and grubby and needs a clean!"

"Wait!" I said. And I showed Daddy
the label under Bear's bottom.

DO NOT WASH THIS BEAR

But Daddy still didn't listen.

He popped Bear in the **washing machine**.

Bear whizzed and whirled.

Round and round.

Soapy and sloshy.

Foamy and frothy.

Then Daddy opened the door. Oh no!
Washing Bear was a **big mistake** . . .

Bear was different.
He waved at me.

He winked
at me.

He blew a **raspberry**!

"Look, Daddy!" I yelled. But Daddy was too busy looking for lost socks to see what Bear was up to.

Suddenly, Bear jumped out of the wash basket and ran up the stairs.

"Stop!" I said.

But Bear
didn't listen . . .

He bounced into the bathroom
and started making bubbles.

Big bubbles.

"Stop!" I shouted.

But Bear didn't listen . . .

SOAP

He ran into my bedroom
and made it snow.

Too much **snow!**

"Stop!
Achoo!"
I sneezed.

But Bear didn't listen . . .

Bear roly-polied down the hall,
jumped on the cat and took
off down the stairs . . .

"Stop that bear!"
I hollered.

But Daddy
had so much
washing, he
couldn't see what
Bear was up to!

CRASH!

Just then the front
door opened.

"Mummy!"
I cried.

Mummy looked at Bear.

Then she looked at Daddy and shook her head.

"You should have read the label!" she said.

"DO NOT WASH THIS BEAR!"

Mummy grabbed Bear
by the ears and
carried him, kicking
and grumbling, out
to the garden . . .

. . . and pegged him
on the line to dry.

Very soon, Bear was back to his old self again.
Daddy said Bear smelled better now.

But then he picked up Rabbit.

"Poo-eee," Daddy said. "Rabbit needs a wash!"

"NoooOOOOO!"

I shouted as I pointed to the label . . .